ALL THE SCARS WE CANNOT SEE

HEART OF A WOUNDED HERO

SADIE KING

ALL THE SCARS WE CANNOT SEE

HEART OF A WOUNDED HERO

Man is not meant to live alone. He becomes dangerous, possessive, protective of what's his. And she is all mine...

Since retiring from the military, I don't like human company.

Until I meet Emily, my new neighbor.

She's as damaged as I am and running from her own demons.

When they catch up with her, I must fight my own inner darkness to protect the woman I love.

But two broken hearts don't always make a whole…

All the Scars We Cannot See is an instalove mountain man romance featuring a scarred ex-military recluse and a curvy girl on the run who steals his heart.

SEMPER FI & AMERICA'S FUND

Semper Fi & America's Fund cares for the U.S.A.'s critically wounded ill, and injured service members and military families. Supporting all branches of the U.S. Armed Forces, they provide one-on-one case management, connection, and lifetime support.

Today. Tomorrow. Together.

The Heart of the Wounded Hero series was created to pay tribute to and raise awareness of our wounded heroes.

Each of the over eighty authors involved have contributed time, money, and stories to the cause. These love stories are inspiring and uplifting, showing the sacrifice of our veterans but also giving them the happily ever after they deserve.

By increasing awareness through our books, we believe we can in a small part help the wounded heroes that have sacrificed so much.

To see all the books in the series and to support Semper Fi & America's Fund, visit www.heartofawoundedhero.com

Copyright © 2022 by Sadie King.

All rights reserved.

No part of this book may be reproduced in any form or by any electronic or mechanical means, including information storage and retrieval systems, without written permission from the author, except for the use of brief quotations in a book review.

Cover designed by Cormer Covers

This is a work of fiction. Any resemblance to actual events, companies, locales or persons living or dead, are entirely coincidental.

www.authorsadieking.com

1
SAM

Dust kicks up from the gravel and swirls around the car as it makes its way along the access road. Burgundy red Corolla. Early model hatchback with a dent in the passenger side door and one side mirror hanging off. It's barely roadworthy and certainly not the kind of vehicle suitable for the roads this far up the mountain.

Picking up my binoculars, I try to make out the driver. Through the dust haze, I can tell they're a woman with long dark hair and wearing wide sunglasses.

Probably a lost tourist out looking for an adventure off the beaten track. Only the back seat is loaded with belongings, making the back end of the car sag under the weight.

She must be lost. There's only my place and the abandoned farm up this road. It's the reason I bought this cabin. No neighbors. No tourists. Just me and the mountain.

Until this beat-up little car turned up on my access road.

I guess she'll figure out soon enough that this road doesn't lead anywhere. Then she'll turn around and go home.

Even as I'm thinking it, the car starts to slow down. It turns into the driveway to the abandoned farm. She'll turn around there and head back the way she came, back to the tourist trails where she belongs.

Only she doesn't. The car turns all the way into the driveway and stops just outside the farmhouse.

The driver's door opens, and a pair of long, thick legs step out. I adjust the focus on the binoculars to take her in.

She's got her back to me, giving a good view of her curvy hourglass figure, wide hips encased in ass-hugging leggings, and long dark hair hanging over her shoulders.

My blood rushes to my dick, and it's suddenly hard to breathe.

"Damn."

I pull the binoculars off my eyes and turn my head away, trying to get my racing pulse under control. It's been a long time since a woman had that kind of effect on me. Not that I get the chance to see many women these days.

Running a hand through my hair, I take a swig of the cool beer sitting next to me on the coffee table.

It does nothing to quench my thirst.

As soon as I raise the binoculars and train them on the woman, my throat goes bone dry.

Her hips sway as she walks to the front door of the house. That old farm has been empty since I moved in three years ago, so if she's expecting to call on someone, she'll be disappointed.

But she doesn't ring the bell. Instead she reaches for her keys and jiggles the lock. A moment later, she pushes open the front door and disappears into the house.

"Damn," I mutter for the second time as I lower the binoculars.

Looks like I got myself a new neighbor.

2
EMILY

The door creaks as I push it open and step into the house. It's stuffy, and there's some acrid smell that makes my nostrils burn. I cover my nose with my sleeve and make my way through the entryway and into the living room.

A coffee table covered in a thick layer of dust sits askew in the middle of the room. There's a worn sofa with the stuffing pulled out, as if some small animal has made its nest there—which would explain the smell.

Dust floats in the air, caught in the late afternoon sun streaming through the dirty window. As I look out the window, my breath catches in my throat.

It's beautiful. There're farm buildings scattered near the house and, beyond them, a line of trees that drops off over a ridge, the whole valley laid out below.

A tingle runs up my spine. It's covered in dust and there may be small animals living in the sofa, but this place is all mine.

Too bad I have to sell it.

I find the breaker in the hallway, and there's an anxious

moment before I work up the courage to flick on the electricity.

The place hums to life, and I let out a deep breath. At least I'll have light and heating.

Next, I find the water and turn on the mains. The pump shakes to life, and for a moment, I think it's not going to work. But then water comes spluttering out of the faucet.

It's surprising how happy that makes me feel. I've got power, and I've got water. I suppose internet is too much to ask for, but at least I've got the essentials.

Making my way through the house, I assess the condition of each room, making a mental note of what needs doing to make the place presentable.

It's been a long time since the farmhouse was lived in. Though apart from needing a good clean and pest control, it doesn't look to be in terrible shape.

If I was staying, I'd pull up the carpets and completely redecorate. But all I need to do is get it in condition to sell. Let the new owners do the rest.

Upstairs, I find the master bedroom. The mattress is covered in dust, but thankfully it doesn't look like any mice have nested here. Upending the mattress, I give it a good whack, sending dust motes into the air and making me double over in a coughing fit.

While the dust settles, I head outside to get my things from the car.

I only bring in what I need for the night: my essentials and my sleeping bag. Until I can get the place cleaned up, I don't want to put lots of stuff down on the dirty floor.

Not that I brought much with me. I didn't want to draw attention to my leaving, so it was a case of packing the essentials, loading the car quickly, and sneaking off in the predawn darkness.

I glance at my watch. They'll have noticed by now that I

haven't turned up for my shift. But that in itself isn't cause for concern. It might not be until tomorrow when I don't turn up again that anyone will realize I've left town.

I breathe out heavily. I'm counting on this place being remote enough that they won't find me for a while.

As I'm getting my things out of the car, I notice a structure on the side of the hill. Up the road a little is a cabin built into the mountain and surrounded by foliage.

It's strange but also comforting to know that even in the middle of nowhere, I have a neighbor.

I squint up at the cabin, but there's no sign of movement, only a wide, empty window with the reflection of the setting sun on it. I'm about to look away when something glints, like glass catching in the sunlight.

It seemed to come from the porch, which is mostly in shadow. As I strain to see, it happens again. A glint of light catching on glass.

It seems I do have a neighbor.

Turning quickly, I go inside the house and lock the door behind me.

3
SAM

In the years I've lived on Maple Mountain, that old farmhouse has sat abandoned. An empty shell; a dark stain on the horizon. Now, there's a warm glow coming from within that looks inviting.

I adjust the focus on my binoculars as the woman moves between the rooms upstairs. There're no curtains, so I can see her perfect form as she bends over to inspect furnishings and dusts off old bedding.

The place must be a mess. I've never seen anyone go in. When I bought my cabin, I was told a guy owned the farm. He used to live up here most of the year on his own. I don't know anything else about him and didn't think to ask.

It was enough to know my nearest neighbor had abandoned the mountain. Now I wish I'd found out more.

The sun's just about set when I finally lower my binoculars. I don't usually watch people like this, but this woman has awakened something in me that I haven't felt for a long time.

My chickens need tending to, and after feeding them, I make myself a fresh omelet and some toast.

I'm sitting in my comfy chair reading a novel when I hear a sweet noise carrying across the valley.

It takes me a moment to realize what it is. And when I do, I lunge for the binoculars.

She's singing. The sweetest sound I've ever heard. She probably doesn't realize it carries on the night air.

Putting the binoculars to my eyes, I scan the dark house until I find her lit up through an upstairs window.

She's got her hair tied back in a scarf, and she must have found a broom somewhere because she's sweeping the floor. I adjust the binoculars so I can study her face.

Some of her hair has gotten loose and falls in wispy strands that frame her oval face. Her lips are plump, and I stare at them, unable to take my eyes away as she sings, her perfect mouth forming the sweet notes.

Her voice is like an angel's, all sweetness and bright and like things too good for my ears to hear.

I don't know how long I watch her. There're no curtains in the house, and she goes from room to room, wiping surfaces and sweeping up debris.

I know I should look away, but I'm drawn to her.

The moon is high in the sky and the singing has stopped by the time she sets down her cleaning gear. I've kept my lights off so if she were to look over this way, all she'd see is my dark cabin. She'll never know I was watching her.

She mustn't know because as I watch, her hands slide under her t-shirt and peel it off. Her back is to me, so all I see is the pale skin of her back and a tattoo under her left shoulder blade, half-concealed by her bra.

Then she turns around. My breath catches in my throat, and my dick twitches.

Her breasts are framed in a black lacey bra. There's a perfect v of cleavage, and I long to run my hand down the crease, slide my fingers under the lace, and feel the weight of those heavy breasts.

The bra unhooks, and her breasts fall free, showing dark nipples that pucker in the cool night air. My cock hardens, and a volt of electricity goes through my body.

She's only got her top off for an instant, but it's enough. I know the image of her tits will be embedded in my brain for eternity.

She slides a loose t-shirt on, covering her breasts. But my cock is rock hard.

I slide it out of my pants and give it a long, slow tug. It's been a long time since I've been with a woman, and my new neighbor has awakened something in me that I thought was long dead.

A longing for company—for her company.

I came to the mountain to escape humanity, and for the first time in a long time, I've seen a human I want to be around.

Long after her lights go out, I sit in the dark, with an ache in my cock and the image of her prefect breasts in my mind.

4
EMILY

The place looks only slightly better in the morning. I found an old rag to wipe away the thick layers of dust and an old broom, but I need to get proper cleaning supplies.

Breakfast is a bowl of cereal with long life milk. I won't trust the fridge until I've given it a good cleaning out.

As I crunch on my Cheerios, I make a list of the supplies I need from town.

I haven't had a chance to take a proper tour of the farm buildings to see what state they're in and what repairs need doing.

That will have to wait. Today, I need to make the house livable.

I'm writing a list of cleaning supplies when there's a knock at the front door.

My pen skitters across the table and lands on the floor as my heart rate shoots up a notch.

They can't have found me already.

With trembling hands, I reach for the small knife I keep in my purse.

There're no curtains in this place, so I press myself against the wall as I quietly approach the door.

"Who is it?"

I try to keep my voice steady. Confidence is half the show, as my old colleagues used to say.

"It's your neighbor."

The deep, guttural voice sends a shiver down my body that isn't unpleasant. The voice is raspy, like it doesn't get used much, and definitely male. Not a voice I recognize.

I remember the glint of something catching in the light yesterday evening from the cabin on the hill. They must have seen me arrive.

A shiver goes down my spine, and I shake the fear away. There's no way someone way out here on the side of a mountain would know who I was—or what I'm running from.

"What do you want?" I call through the door.

Still, it doesn't hurt to be cautious.

There's silence on the other side of the door. I lean forward, wondering about the man on the other side of the wood. When he speaks again, his voice is less raspy, lighter.

"I want to welcome you to the neighborhood."

I let out a breath I didn't know I was holding. Here I am being super paranoid, and this guy just wants to be neighborly.

Keeping the chain on the latch, I open the door and peer through.

He's as rugged as the deep voice suggests. Over six feet tall with shaggy hair and a beard to match. Lines spread out from his dark eyes, giving him a haunted look. I'd say he's at least in his late thirties, maybe older.

When he sees me, his eyes widen and the lines turn upward to match the smile that's peeping out from behind his beard.

This guy's a regular mountain man. Rough and rugged. My heartbeat increases, but not from fear this time. Just looking at this hulk of a man makes my skin pucker and my core turn to liquid.

"Hi." His voice is a low rumble that sends a shock wave all the way to my core. "I'm Sam. I live in the cabin up the hill."

He extends a hand, a shy smile on his face. He must be aware of how ridiculous this is. This being me peering at him through a slit in the door. I get the feeling he's kind of laughing at me, but in a friendly way.

I tear my gaze way from him to scan the surrounding area. All I can see is my car parked on an otherwise empty driveway.

He's not one of the thugs sent by Mika, that's for sure.

I shut the door briefly as I undo the chain. When I open it again, his hand is still extended, and I take it.

"I'm…" The shock of his hand on mine stops me short. His hands are callused, rough against my skin and warm. So warm it sends tingles all the way up my forearm.

Sam tilts his head, looking at me expectantly. "I'm…" I pause again, and he raises an eyebrow. But I don't know what to call myself here. I've been going by a fake name for so long, it's become part of my identity. An identity I want to leave behind.

"I'm Emily."

It's been so long since I used my real name that it sounds foreign in my mouth.

"Emily," Sam repeats. I like the way his deep voice says it. My real name is definitely growing on me.

"Yeah. Emily."

I drop his hand and feel the loss of his warmth immediately.

"Welcome to Maple Mountain, Emily."

I feel sure he's going to ask me about myself, and I put my arms around my chest, suddenly feeling vulnerable. I'm not ready to answer any questions. I haven't prepared any lies.

Luckily, Sam isn't the nosey neighbor type.

"You need help with anything—anything at all—you come see me, okay?"

The kindness of his words makes my eyes sting. I look away quickly. The last thing I want to do is cry in front of my hot new neighbor. But I haven't had much kindness in my life, especially not from strangers.

"Thank you," I say, looking down as I scuff my feet over a loose board so he can't see my eyes.

"I'm just up the hill. There's a path by the big tree that cuts through." He indicates a large cedar tree, and I can make out a break in the foliage where the path must be.

"I can be down here in less than a minute if you need me fast. Just holler."

I glance up at him quickly. It's as if he knows I may be in need of a strong mountain man at some point to fight off my old associates. But his face remains neutral.

I guess he just means if I need to borrow sugar or something.

"Thanks, Sam."

"I best be going. Just wanted to introduce myself is all."

He hops on his foot awkwardly, and I get the feeling this mountain man isn't used to human company.

I watch him walk away, and he turns at the path and gives me a wave. The friendly gesture makes me feel lighter. I'm not completely on my own out here, and that's a relief.

5
SAM

*E*mily's running from something, that's for sure. The way she cautiously opened the door and the furtive looks over my shoulder let me know that. I just hope she isn't into anything that could get her hurt.

She's even prettier up close. Seeing those plump lips only inches away rather than through a lens has got me hot and sweaty.

Back at my cabin, I watch Emily's house. It's becoming a habit that I can't shake.

It's not long before she gets in her car. As she buckles up, an anxious gnawing starts in my stomach. Emily might not be safe. Whatever she's running from might catch up to her if I'm not watching and ready to protect her.

She's into something bad. She's scared of something. Even though I just met her, she's on my mountain, and I feel responsible for her.

Without thinking about it too much, I grab my keys and head to my pickup. I let her get a bit down the road before I follow.

It's a good fifteen minutes to Maple Falls town center.

There's not much here, and I pull over at the end of the main road to watch Emily.

She's only in the grocery store for ten minutes, and I'm guessing it doesn't have everything she needs because she gets back in her beat-up car and heads out of town.

I follow at a safe distance. I know where she's going. The nearest proper town is Maple Springs about an hour away. It's where we all go when we need the supplies that our little mountain town can't offer.

My hands go clammy on the steering wheel as we approach Maple Springs. It's been a long time since I came into this town, and I feel the anxiousness start in my hands.

As we approach the edge of the township, where there're rows of neat houses and people walking along the street, my palms are sweaty and my fingers tap the steering wheel nervously.

By the time I'm following her down Main Street, my right leg is jiggling and my chest feels tight.

Taking deep breaths, I try to calm my nerves and focus on Emily's red Corolla. She parks next to a bargain store, and I pull over across the road near a clump of trees so she can't see me if she looks this way.

There's a sound like machine-gun fire, and my neck snaps around as I duck in my seat. A group of women walks past laughing loudly, their mouths thrown open as they cackle over some joke. It's just laughter, I tell myself. Just laughter.

Getting my breathing under control, I watch Emily go into the shop. A little while later, she comes out with bags full of what looks like cleaning supplies, with bottles of disinfectant and a new mop poking out the top of the bag.

She loads it into her trunk, then heads down the street.

I expect her to go into the hardware store, so I'm surprised when she goes into the electronic shop.

It's a glass-fronted shop, and I grab my binoculars to see

what she's looking at. She's speaking to a sales assistant, and he reaches for a box on one of the shelves. Security cameras.

If she's buying security cameras on her first day here, she's definitely twitchy about something. I understand a woman living on her own wants to feel protected, but it looks like she's buying more than one.

My mind whirls as I watch her make the purchase. Who exactly is Emily, and what is she running from?

It only makes my urge to protect her stronger.

It's a busy Saturday morning, and she ducks into Candy's Cafe. It's supposed to have the best cookies in town, but I've never been able to face the crowds that are always there. Just thinking about it makes beads of sweat burst onto my forehead.

I imagine Emily ordering a coffee and wonder what it would be like to sit in a cafe with her, like a normal person, chatting over coffee and cake.

There's a loud bang and I duck down, shielding my head. I'm transported back to Afghanistan—the sound of ripping metal and the acrid smell of burning tires. My eyes squeeze shut, and I count to ten trying to shake the flashback out of my head.

The memory fades, and when I open my eyes, I'm crouched in the bed of the pickup truck, my arm over my head.

If anyone saw me, if Emily saw me like this, she'd think I was mad. A grown man hiding in the cab of his truck all because a car backfired.

I slide up onto the front seat and look around. No one seemed to notice me, or if they did, they're too polite to stare.

There's no way Emily would want to be seen with a guy like me. I'm damaged goods. There's no way I could take her out anywhere nice or be the man she needs.

I don't know what I was thinking following her here. It's

obvious she's scared of something, but how can I protect her when I can't even sort myself out?

Putting the truck in gear, I pull out of the parking space. I'm not fit for human company. It's better to retreat back to my mountain where I belong.

6

EMILY

The rickety barn door creaks as I swing it open.

The windows are boarded over, making it hard to see, and when I flick on the light switch, nothing happens.

I guess the intact electrics don't extend this far.

Propping the door open with a piece of wood, I venture into the barn, going slowly to give my eyes time to adjust to the dark.

There is debris strewn over the concrete floor, and broken glass from a window lies on the ground. But the wooden beams holding it up are in good condition and the building looks sound.

It would make a lovely barn conversion. It could be a homestay, or a spa retreat, or a meditation center.

My spine tingles at the possibilities. The surrounding area itself is so peaceful already, with the quiet mountain and view of the valley. This would be the perfect place for a retreat of some kind.

When Dad left me this place, my first thought was to clean it up enough to find a buyer and sell it. But now, as I run my hand over the old wooden beams, I can imagine how the old farm would look with a makeover.

The barn could be where the guests stay, and some of the smaller farm buildings could be treatment rooms. I'd build a covered outdoor area with a fire pit for relaxation and put in some outdoor hot tubs.

As I carefully climb the ladder to the mezzanine, I wonder how much it would take to convert this place into a beauty retreat. Somewhere for weary women—and men, I suppose— to come and rest for a while. Somewhere to get their nails done and enjoy a luxurious massage with a dip in the hot tubs.

Not that I have any experience in running a place like that or converting an old farm into anything. I sigh heavily.

It's just a pipe dream. Better to keep on my path of finding a buyer. Let someone else do the hard work. With the money from the sale, it should be enough to pay back my debts and find a quiet place on my own somewhere.

The one good thing Dad did for me was leaving this old farm. I sigh again.

If only he'd told me about it before he passed away. I could have had it sold and used the money instead of getting into debt.

Typical of my dad not to think about something like that, even while he took my money for his treatment.

My chest tightens as it always does when I think of him.

He was a complex man, and I can't blame him entirely for being the way he was or leaving me and Mom alone like he did. But life sure as hell would have been a whole lot easier if he had stuck around.

After inspecting the farm buildings, it's time to set up the security system.

Three cameras were all I could afford in the end. I have to make the money last until I can get this place sold, and I've got no idea how long that will be.

Grabbing the property plans that were thrust upon me by the attorney executing Dad's will, I walk the perimeter of my land.

On one side is the road and driveway, which is the most likely way anyone will approach, so that definitely needs a camera pointing at it.

On the left side is the hill with Sam's cabin at the top. Because of the steepness and the fact there's a dwelling on it, I doubt anyone would try to approach from that way.

The other two edges are framed by trees. It's all dense bush leading to pine forest, not easy to get through without a path—but not impossible.

Getting out a ladder, I fix the cameras to the roof, with one looking to the road and the other two looking out to the back corners of the property.

I'm fixing the last camera when I feel a tingle down my spine and the hairs on the back of my neck stand on end. I look up quickly, expecting to see someone, but there's just the silent mountain.

Feeling uneasy, I head inside. Since I've been here, I've had this feeling like I'm being watched. I'm sure it's just the paranoia of being on the run from my debtors, but sometimes the feeling is so acute, I have to go inside.

There's a monitor that the cameras connect to, and I switch between each camera, my senses on high alert. But there's nothing there.

I let out a deep breath. It's probably just a mountain goat or something watching me from the forest.

Even so, I double lock the doors and place my knife under my pillow before turning in for the night.

7
SAM

It's been almost two weeks since my new neighbor moved in. Despite my resolve to stay away, I'm drawn to the lights peeping through the trees, the soft glow of her house. In the evenings, I watch the house, straining my eyes through the binoculars, hoping to catch a glimpse of the full-figured Emily.

During the day, I watch the activity around her property, observing what she does and the care she's taking to clean the place up. I watch every time she stops for a break, crouching on the grass with her hair tumbling behind her.

I'm checking in, I tell myself. Making sure she's safe from whatever it is she's running from.

But if I'm honest with myself, that's only part of the truth. There's something about Emily that makes me hungry. She's ignited a craving inside, a need to observe her, to find out all about her. It's impossible to pull my gaze away from Emily.

I can't stop looking her. Her full lips, the way she leans one hand on her hips as she stares out at the valley, the curve of her thighs as she sweeps the yard.

After the incident in town, my dark mood lasted for several

days. It was a struggle to get out of bed, to find motivation to do anything.

I've had dark episodes ever since my time in the military. They can come on suddenly, triggered by a car backfiring, or a crowd of people pushing too close, or the smell of burning rubber.

It was only Emily's singing that helped me start to feel human again. That sweet voice pierced through the darkness, melting it away like butter.

Just as suddenly as the blackness descended, it was gone. I pulled myself out of bed, showered, tended to the chickens, and got on with life, feeling almost normal again.

It's typical of my dark moods to be like that. They come and go, and there's nothing I can do about it. When I first moved here, they were worse. But there's something healing about the mountain and its quietness and open space.

Slowly, my mind started to heal. It's not perfect, but I'm a damn sight better than I was when I first left the military. When I was a broken man.

Drawing my binoculars to my eyes, I scan the property, looking for my pretty songbird. She's in one of the outbuildings today. Over the last few days, I've watched her work through the buildings, cleaning them one by one.

I can't see into this particular building, but there's a bucket and mop leaning against the side of the whitewashed wall and the door's propped open.

With the knowledge that Emily is there, going about her tasks and humming to herself—happy and safe—a feeling of calm washes over me. I may be too damaged for Emily, but just knowing she's close by brings a sense of comfort to me.

I lower the binoculars and place them next to my coffee mug on the table. Taking a sip of coffee, I open my latest paperback. While Emily works, I'll sit and read in companionable silence. She may not know I'm here, but her presence is a comfort I've gotten used to.

A few minutes later, movement along the road catches my eye.

A cloud of dust moves down the road. A car kicking up the gravel. Reaching for the binoculars, I make out a bright yellow souped-up Chevy Camaro with tinted windows and a spoiler that's as big as the trunk. A car like that's got no business being on the side of a mountain.

A prickle starts low in my spine. This isn't right.

The car slows down as it approaches Emily's driveway.

Whoever Emily's been running from has just caught up with her.

8
EMILY

I'm humming as I sweep the debris from one of the outbuildings into a pile on the floor so it can be be scooped up and taken away.

This building's concrete with whitewashed walls and one empty window frame. It would be just big enough for a treatment room of some sort or a one person cabin. Whatever the new developers want to do with it.

I've spoken to a real estate agent and they think it will sell easily, but they won't touch the place until I get it cleaned up. They need the photos to look good, I guess, so people can imagine what they could do with the place.

I pause for a minute and lean on the broom, thinking about how nice it could look: the walls freshly painted; a pane of glass in the window; a lamp giving soft mood lighting.

That's when I hear the sound of a car.

I've been here nearly two weeks and the only other car I've heard is Sam's pickup, and this doesn't sound like his engine.

We're the only two dwellings on this road, so either this car's lost or they're here to see one of us. And Sam doesn't seem like the kind of guy who gets many guests.

With a knot forming in my stomach, I peer out of the window, waiting for the car to come into view.

The mop and bucket leaning outside the building give my location away. Darting to the door, I grab the mop and bucket, pulling them inside, just as a car pulls into the driveway.

My heart leaps into my throat. I'd recognize that souped-up Camaro anywhere. With my heart hammering in my chest, I watch Mika step out of the passenger side.

It was only a matter of time before he found me, but I thought I'd have a few months, not a few weeks.

He's wearing his trademark tight trousers and white snakeskin shoes. His hair is slicked back, his face pulled into a tight expression.

I crouch down, out of sight of the window, with my hands shaking. My knife is in the house. I can visualize where I left it tucked under my pillow.

Two weeks on the mountain has made me complacent, and now I'm stuck here without a weapon.

"Krystle!" calls Mika, using the other name I'm known as.

I bite the inside of my cheek to stop myself from calling out.

"We know you're here."

We? I risk a peek through the window and see another man getting out of the car. It's Lionel, one of the thugs from the club.

He's a beast of a man, tall and wide. As he steps out of the car, he tilts his head, cracking his neck. The sound makes me shudder.

If Mika's brought Lionel with him, then he hasn't come for tea and cookies.

"Krystle."

Mika calls out again as he bangs on the front door. The noise makes my knees knock together, and I tighten my grip on the broom handle, squeezing my eyes shut.

"We don't want to hurt you. We just want our money."

There's the sound of bones cracking again, which I guess is Lionel limbering up, and it tells me that Mika's lying.

They could harm me out here—really harm me—and no one would know. I realize how stupid I've been by leaving the knife in the house. My grip on the broom tightens. It's the only weapon I've got.

"She's not home."

I jump at the sound of the gravelly voice almost as much as Mika does. Sam's strolling down the drive looking as solid as one of the forest's trees, casually holding his axe in one hand.

Relief floods me.

I've not seen my reclusive neighbor since that first day he introduced himself, and it's good to see him again. Really good.

Mika gives Sam a once-over.

"Who the fuck are you?"

Sam doesn't drop eye contact. Mika intimidates most people, but he's probably never come across a burly mountain man swinging an axe before.

"A friendly neighbor."

Mika takes a step toward Sam, his anger coming out in his voice.

"You expect me to believe she's not here when her shithole of a car's parked right outside?"

Sam never takes his eyes off Mika. "She went for a walk."

Mika snorts. "Then I'll wait until she comes home."

Sam nods slowly, casually letting the axe swing in his hand. "I'll wait with you."

Lionel cracks his knuckles again, and Sam turns his head to look at him.

There's something hard about Sam, something dark and wild that I see on his face. He's not scared of Lionel; he's not scared of a fight.

Lionel and Mika must sense it, too, because after a few moments, Mika gives an exaggerated sigh.

"We'll come back another time."

"I suggest you do."

Mika points his finger at Sam and takes a step forward so he's almost poking him in the chest.

"But you tell Krystle that I want my money back by the end of the week. Or we're coming back for another visit, and this one won't be so pleasant."

My knees give out at that. I've seen what Mika does to people who cross him. I was stupid to think I could run. Stupid to think he wouldn't find me here.

My hands are shaking so badly that I let go of the broom. It crashes to the floor, and three sets of eyes turn to the outbuildings.

I duck away from the window, sinking to the floor.

"What was that?"

I hear footsteps approach the building, and I back away from the door as they get closer and closer.

"That's probably the bear we got living around here."

"There're no bears here." It's Mika's voice, and he's getting closer.

"Have a look if you like. She's been nesting in that building, keeping her cubs warm."

The footsteps stop, and I can imagine Mika's snakeskin shoes hesitating on the gravel, trying to weigh what Sam's saying. A city boy trying to remember what he knows about bears.

"She's a big one for a female," Sam says good-naturedly. "Only comes out looking for food, or if her cubs are threatened."

The footsteps move away quickly, and then there's the sound of two car doors slamming.

"You tell Krystle what we said, all right? We'll be back. And next time, I'll bring a shotgun for the bear."

The car engine fires up, and tires squeal as they speed off. It seems Mika can't get out of here fast enough.

I crouch in the dim light, my teeth chattering with fright.

Footsteps approach. These ones are strong and confident. The door pulls open, and Sam peers in, a look of concern on his face.

"They're gone, little bear."

I register the words, but I can't move. My body's shaking. I try to speak, but nothing comes out. Sam's expression turns to fear.

Then he's by my side.

"Emily, you're in shock."

Sam's arm slides under my legs, and he lifts me up. The last thing I remember is how warm and solid Sam feels as he carries me out of the building.

9
SAM

*E*mily's shaking as I lift her off the concrete floor. Her body presses against mine, and I carry her across the lawn and to the path that leads up to my place.

Those bastards have given her such a fright that she's gone into shock.

My training kicks in. I know I have to get her warm as quickly as possible. I jog up the path with Emily in my arms and push open the door to my cabin.

She's still trembling when I set her down on the couch. I grab a woolen blanket from my bed and wrap it around her shoulders.

"You're going to be okay, Emily."

She looks up at me with wide eyes. Her mouth opens, but I shush her.

"Don't try to speak. I'm going to take your pulse."

Trying to ignore the citrus scent of her body wash and the softness of her skin, I press my fingers against her throat, searching for the beat of her pulse. It flutters weakly under my fingers. Too weakly.

ALL THE SCARS WE CANNOT SEE

Pulling the blankets tighter around her, I pull Emily close to me and put my arm around her.

My body heat should help revive her, and I try to ignore the feel of her breasts pressed against me. Her head sinks into my shoulder and her hair falls loose around her shoulders. I tuck loose strands behind her ear. She closes her eyes, and I run my hand over her head, stroking her hair in slow, calming movements.

"It's okay. I'm here for you."

The chattering of her teeth slows, and her breathing starts to regulate.

We stay like this for a few minutes as I feel her shock start to ease.

It's comforting, having my arm wrapped around Emily. She fits perfectly into the crook of my neck, like she belongs there.

Eventually, she raises her head. Her eyes are brighter than they were, and her teeth have stopped chattering.

"What happened to me?" she asks in a croaky voice.

"You went into shock, honey. Those men…"

She looks down, and I don't finish my sentence. It's obvious she doesn't want to talk about it, and she's probably still feeling weak.

I'll need to know about them at some point if I'm to help her, but for now, I just want to make sure she's all right.

"Let me get the fire going."

I take my time stoking the fire while Emily lies on the couch with her eyes closed. She looks vulnerable lying like that, pale and scared.

Whoever those men are, whatever they want from her, they'll have to answer to me first. Emily is mine to protect. I've known that since I first saw her step out of her car and onto my mountain.

The fire gives the room an orange glow, and I watch the

light flicker over Emily's face. I'm not sure if she's asleep, so I go quietly into the kitchen to fix us something to eat.

When I pop my head in to check on her a few minutes later, she's sitting up.

"How you feeling?"

Emily stretches, seeming to mentally check her body.

"Okay. Tired."

She frowns, confused. And I get that. The exhaustion that comes after shock. I've seen it too many times.

"Can I take your pulse again?"

"Sure."

She tilts her head to the side, exposing the delicate skin of her throat.

This time, when I touch her, I'm overwhelmed by our closeness, the smell of her citrus shower gel mixed with the sharpness of cleaning products.

Emily gasps when my fingers brush her throat, and her eyes dart up to find mine.

Her pulse is stronger than before, but still weak. As our eyes lock, I feel it quicken.

Could she be as affected by this close contact as I am? Her lips part, and I'm so close to her mouth I could lean forward just an inch and kiss her.

But she's had a shock. That's all this is. She's still in shock and probably feeling vulnerable and thankful that I saved her. I won't take advantage of that.

I pull my fingers off her neck and stand up. Disappointment flashes across her face, and she turns away to adjust the blanket.

"You need to rest, honey. I'll have some food ready soon."

With my own pulse racing and my dick hard as stone, I retreat to the kitchen.

10
EMILY

The last few hours are a blur.

When I heard Mika's threats, I'm not sure what happened. I think my body shut down.

I thought I was tougher than that. I've had to do things over the past few years that I'm not proud of, and they made me strong. Or so I thought.

But spending these few weeks on this mountain has slit me wide open. I dared to believe I could leave Mika and the club behind for good. And when he came looking for me, the thought of going back to that life was too much.

Sam's been so nice to me I could cry.

He's virtually a stranger, but his steady presence calmed me down—his gentle touch; the smell of fresh wood and coffee as he wrapped me in his arms to stop the shaking.

Now he's looking at me sideways as I shovel bits of omelet into my mouth. I chew slowly, trying not to look like a total pig, but I'm suddenly ravenous.

We're eating off trays as we sit on the couch in front of the fire. Sam's watching me as I eat. I guess he wants to make sure I don't start shaking again.

I vaguely remember him effortlessly picking me up, and I'm not a small girl. I remember his body pressing against mine and shamelessly leaning into him.

Sam's shown nothing but kindness and concern, and he's never once asked me about why I'm in debt or why the hell a man in white snakeskin boots came looking for me.

My heart softens for my protective neighbor. I barely know him, but I already feel safe with Sam. The safest I've ever felt in my life.

"Thank you," I say once I finish chewing.

"No problem. I have some hens out back, so always plenty of eggs for an omelet."

He stands up and takes my empty plate.

"I mean thank you for today."

But he's already disappeared into the kitchen. When he comes back, he's holding an amber colored liquid in a tumbler.

"This'll help," he says.

I take the glass and give it a sniff. My nose crinkles.

"What is that?"

His lips curl up in a smile. "The best Scotch whiskey you can get."

I take a tentative sip. The liquid is like fire scorching my throat, but once it hits my belly, a warm glow starts and spreads right through my bones.

"Not bad." I'm surprised when I say it.

"There's a Scotsman who lives on the mountain, gives me a bottle every now and then."

I raise my eyebrows. Sam doesn't strike me as the type of guy who has many friends.

"Do you know many people on the mountain?"

He shakes his head. "I mostly keep to myself, but there're some good folks who live here."

I take another sip and let the fiery liquid warm me up.

Sam's looking into the fire, swirling his whiskey. And while I don't feel like he's pressuring me, I know he deserves an explanation.

Downing the rest of my glass for courage, I take a deep breath and begin.

"Those men who were here today…"

Sam keeps looking at the fire, and I go on.

"I owe them some money."

"I gathered that."

I bite my lower lip. I don't know if I can tell him all of it. He seems to think I'm a good person. I don't want him to know the truth about me.

"I borrowed money from Mika to pay for my dad's care."

I decide on telling the truth and just leaving out the bits he doesn't need to know.

"This place here"—I indicate across the road, to my run-down farm—"belonged to my dad. I only found out about it at his will reading a few weeks ago."

Sam looks at me, concern on his face.

"I'm sorry."

I shake my head, thinking about the father I barely knew.

"I didn't know my dad well, not until the last few years. He was ex-military."

Sam's head snaps up. I've got his attention now.

"But when he came back from war, he was never the same. I was only a baby and don't remember much, but I know he walked out on me and Mom."

Anger flashes on Sam's face for a moment.

"Mom struggled to raise me on her own, and when she was killed in a car accident…"

I swallow the lump in my throat. I was twelve years old when Mom passed, but I still miss her every single day.

"I wanted to go and live with Dad, but he was hard to track

down and the authorities wouldn't allow it. They didn't think he'd cope, and he didn't push for it."

I shrug. I gave up being angry at my dad long ago. I know he had mental health problems, PTSD that made it hard for him to function. He couldn't have raised me; I know that now.

There were years of foster care while I finished high school. Occasionally, I'd see Dad and he'd make an effort, but he always looked haunted, always anxious. Then he'd disappear for months at a time, not telling me where he was, like he didn't want to be found.

"It wasn't until he got seriously sick that I saw a lot of him."

I look away from the fire, unable to go on for a moment as I remember what it was like being eighteen and ready to go out into the world, finally able to leave foster care behind and strike out on my own.

I remember the disappointment—and then the guilt—that I felt when Dad turned up sick and needing me.

His mental health had deteriorated, and he was committed to a hospital. While in the facility, they diagnosed his cancer.

I don't tell Sam what I did to pay for the medical bills, or how when that wasn't enough, I turned to Mika for a loan.

I thought I'd pay it off easily by working more shifts, but Dad's bills kept coming.

Then Dad passed. Knowing that his suffering was over, I felt relief, then more guilt at my relief.

Then I found out about this place. He'd never told me about the old farm, his own little retreat.

I saw an opportunity. If I can sell the farm, I can pay my debts to Mika and have enough left over to start anew.

Sam's been listening quietly as I talk.

"Your dad sounds like a troubled man." His voice is soft. He stares into the fire. It seems my story has affected him more than I realized.

"He was troubled. The war did that to him. There was no help for him when he came back. He wasn't a bad man. I know that now. He just couldn't cope, and he thought it was better to take himself right out of our lives rather than to stick around and mess things up."

There's a sting in the back of my eyes. I swipe at the tears that threaten, thinking of everything that could have been.

"He didn't realize that would mess me up anyway."

Sam shifts to look at me, his face thrown into shadow by the flickering fire. Without saying a word, his arm goes around me, and I lean into him as if it's the most natural thing in the world.

"You're not messed up, honey." He kisses the top of my head. He doesn't know the whole truth; I can't face telling him all of it.

"Maybe we're all messed up."

Sam pulls away so that he can face me. His finger goes under my chin, and he tilts my head up.

"Maybe we are."

The flickering fire makes his dark eyes glow with golden flecks and throws the deep lines of his face into shadow, making me wonder what demons he's carrying around.

My gaze flicks to his lips, and I wonder what they'd taste like. I long for him to press his lips against mine and give in to this pull between us.

I think he's about to when his hand suddenly drops away and he stands up.

"You'll stay here tonight."

I try to hide my disappointment. "I don't need to stay." Though the thought of being alone in my house makes me shiver.

"I need to watch over you, make sure the shock doesn't come back."

I'm grateful for his protectiveness, and I don't argue again.

"You can take my bed. I'll take the couch."

"Thank you."

Sam's being so kind to me, so generous, even giving up his bed. But I can't help wondering what it would feel like to lie next to him and have his naked body pressed against mine.

11

SAM

While Emily's in the bathroom, I change the sheets on my bed.

My chest is tight as I think about what she just told me. She's been through hell with her dad, and I should know. It's not an easy gig coming out of the military.

But it's not fair that some moneylender took advantage of her.

I lay out a shirt of mine for her to wear. I did offer to go with her to get some things, but she didn't want to go back to the farm. It's obvious she's still a bit shaken and needs to rest.

I wait in the living room for Emily to dress, and when she comes out, my jaw nearly hits the floor. My checkered shirt that she's wearing goes to mid-thigh, showing off her creamy legs. She pulls at it self-consciously, and I try not to stare.

But damn, it's hard.

"You got everything you need for the night?"

I force myself to keep my eyes on hers. If I look at her thighs, or her lips, or the way her breasts are pushed up against the fabric of my shirt, I'm going to lose it.

"Yes, thank you," she says.

"You go to bed then, honey, and get some rest."

"Goodnight."

She retreats to the bedroom, and I let out a big breath. I thought she was hot through my binoculars, but up close, Emily might be the best looking woman I've ever seen.

I pour myself another whiskey and sit in front of the fire.

What she told me about her dad hit home in more ways than she can possibly know. It sounds like she's had a lot of shit to deal with.

And now here I am, another damaged man trying to get into her life. I can't put that on her.

That's why I pulled away when I could have kissed her by the fire. That's why she's in my bed alone while I'm on the couch with only myself for company.

Emily's already had to deal with one broken war veteran in her life; she doesn't need to deal with another.

I knock back another shot of whiskey and let the fiery liquid warm my body and dull my thoughts.

But there is one way I can help Emily. I can find those fuckers who threatened her and make sure she's never bothered by them again.

12
EMILY

Sunlight streams through the window as I wake up the next morning. Stretching lazily, I spread out in the comfy bed, checking in on my body as I stretch.

I fell asleep quickly last night, feeling safer than I have in weeks. Just knowing Sam was in the room next to mine made me feel protected.

Thoughts of Sam make my pulse quicken, and I feel a tug in my core. Lazily, I trail a hand down my body to the place between my legs.

Just thinking about his solid body and the way it felt pressed against me yesterday, his muscles rippling under his shirt—it has me hot all over. I run my palm over my panties and shudder at the sensation.

But I'm in his bed. It wouldn't be right to give myself pleasure without him.

I sigh, thinking about how we almost kissed and how he pulled away.

I could have sworn Sam was into me. The way he looks at me, the way he watches my lips, and the way he cared for me yesterday. But maybe that's it. Maybe he's just a caring guy being a friendly neighbor.

Sliding my hand back on top of the sheets, I climb out of bed.

I pad to the door and tentatively push it open. The smell of coffee hits me, and I hear Sam bustling in the kitchen.

"Morning," I call out.

Only it's not Sam who comes through the door.

A woman appears in the doorway holding a mug of steaming coffee. Her blonde hair is tied up in a messy bun, her tight top showing off a pregnant belly. She gives a wide smile when she sees me.

"You must be Emily."

My stomach drops. Here I am fantasizing about Sam and he's already got a girlfriend. A pregnant one at that.

"Hi," I say awkwardly.

"I'm Jenny. You want coffee?"

She's very chatty for someone who just turned up to find a strange woman in her man's house. I'm not sure I'd be so friendly.

"Sure," I say.

"This one's decaf." She wrinkles her nose up. "The first thing I'm doing once this one arrives is having a proper coffee."

She rubs her belly as she says it and pauses as the baby kicks against her hand.

"Ahh, he's kicking a lot today."

The serene look on her face causes a pang in my chest. I wonder if I'll ever get to feel that one day, a baby growing in my belly. It doesn't seem likely with the way my life's going.

"Sam had to go out for a bit. He asked me to stay with you."

I don't know what to say to this. It seems odd that the girlfriend would want me to stay and not kick me out.

"I'll go back to my place."

She shakes her head. "Strict instructions to keep you here."

This is some extreme mountain hospitality. I mean, I'm wearing her boyfriend's shirt, isn't she a little bit worried?

"I'm just across the road."

Jenny claps her hands together. "We heard someone had moved into the old farm."

That's interesting to know. Here I was thinking I was hiding away, but it seems the whole mountain knows about me. No wonder Mika was able to track me down. Stupid of me to think he wouldn't.

"We're up that way a bit." She indicates out the window. "Even further up the mountain than you are."

She leans in conspiratorially. "Must be something about the mountain that attracts ex-military types. The more secluded a place, the better."

She's smiling as if I know what she's talking about, and her expression changes when she sees my confusion.

"My husband's ex-military too."

Relief floods me more than I'd like to admit.

Jenny has a husband. She's not Sam's girlfriend.

Now that that's established, I find myself quite liking Jenny. She's hard not to like with her friendly smile and good-natured chattiness.

"Your husband?"

"My husband Rowan. Sam called him this morning, asked if he'd come sit with you 'til he got back."

I'm nodding along, but all I feel is relief that she's not Sam's girlfriend.

"He said you'd had a shock last night." She says it good-naturedly. She's not prying, and I relax a little bit more. Jenny isn't here to find out my story. She's just here to keep me company.

"I told Rowan I'd go. If you got a shock yesterday, you'd get more of one today waking up to find my husband in the house."

She laughs, but it's said with affection. "He's even bigger than Sam. And hairier, if you can believe it." She shakes her head, chuckling to herself. "These mountain men come up here and let themselves go. Not that we'd have it any other way of course. We don't see much of Sam, but Rowan knows him from the military, so they have a beer together sometimes."

I suddenly realize what she's been saying, and it's like a light bulb going off in my head.

"Sam's military?"

My chest constricts. He never told me that. I guess I never asked. No wonder he was so shaken by the story about my dad.

"Ex-military. I think he was in the Army. Doesn't speak about it much. None of them do."

Jenny trails off when she sees my expression.

"You didn't know?"

"No." I shake my head slowly. "I don't know much about Sam, really."

I realize that's an understatement. I know he's kind and gentle and makes me feel safe, but I know nothing about who he is or what his life's like.

Jenny indicates the couch, and I take a seat next to her. Her hand goes to my shoulder. It's comforting.

"I don't know Sam's background exactly…" She pauses as if she doesn't know if she should go on. "But from what Rowan's said, it doesn't sound like he's had a good time since leaving."

I think about Sam living up here alone in the cabin opposite where my father used to live.

"Do a lot of ex-military live on the mountain?"

Jenny sips her coffee before she answers. "I think it's a good place to heal, if you need healing. And there's a lot of men who need healing."

I think about my dad. That was definitely true of him. He needed to heal, but he didn't know how. My gaze goes out the window to the trees surrounding us and the valley below.

Just being here must have brought my dad some solace, and it must be the same for Sam.

"I'll put another pot of coffee on. The real stuff this time."

Jenny gets up, bringing the conversation to a close.

I get it. It's not her place to tell me about Sam's wounds, but that doesn't stop me from wondering about him and what he's carrying on those broad shoulders—and if the mountain is healing him more than it healed my dad.

13

SAM

The neon sign flashes against the gloomy afternoon sky. Even at one in the afternoon, there's music pumping in the club and patrons coming in and out.

It didn't take much to track down Mika once I had his license plate. I have connections, ex-military friends who are now in the police force, who will help a guy when he needs it.

Now I'm sitting outside the Pelican Bar in Seattle where the fluorescent green sign promises "Girls Girls Girls."

An uneasy feeling has settled in my gut ever since my ex-Army buddy rang through with this address for me.

I want to believe that Emily knows Mika some other way, but the truth is she probably worked here.

The thought causes a pain in my chest. That girl has been through hell, and her having to make a living this way to look after her old man breaks my heart.

I swear to God that if I can do anything good in this world, it will be to get Emily away from this scene for good.

A car door slams, making me jump. My pulse is already racing, and I take a few deep breaths to bring it under control.

Driving through the city, being surrounded by so many

people and vehicles, has made my anxiety go through the roof. My palms are sweaty, and my heartbeat races along at breakneck speed.

There's the sound of a man laughing, and I squeeze my eyes shut tight.

How can people be enjoying themselves here when all I can think about is the noise of battle? Every thump reminds me of gunfire; every laugh, the cackle of a machine gun; every car could be carrying an IED.

"Come on, man. Get it together."

I breathe in hard and exhale slowly, searching my mind for something positive to focus on. An image of Emily comes into my head: how she looked on that first day I saw her, with her hair tied back and her lips parted as she sang to herself.

I force my mind to focus on Emily as I take a few more breaths. Slowly, the ringing in my ears fades, my heartbeat calms, and I feel the knot in my stomach ease.

I open my eyes.

I'm just a guy sitting in a pickup truck in a parking lot. There's nothing else here. And if I want to help my sweet little songbird, I need to pull myself together and go inside that club.

Wiping my sweaty palms on my jeans, I do one last calming breath before I open the car door.

Inside the club, the music is so loud I can barely think. The bass thumps through my body, causing me to tense up all over again. Sweat breaks out on my forehead, and I clench my fists, my nails digging into my palms until the feeling passes.

On a podium in the middle of the room are two poles, each with a girl swirling around them. A handful of men watch from the side with hungry eyes.

A flash of anger jolts through me. Emily worked here. On this stage. With the same men ogling her.

My fists clench, and a vein throbs in my neck. I'd like to

slam my fist into every man here when I think about them watching Emily like this.

"What can I get you?"

A waitress with a voice like honey looks up at me from under lowered lashes. She's offering me more than a drink, but I'm not here for a private dance. The anger coursing through my veins seems to have banished the anxiety, and I roll with that.

"Where's Mika?"

The sweet look falls off her face as she realizes I'm not a paying customer.

"He's not here."

She turns away and makes her way slowly down the end of the bar. I watch as she pulls back a curtain and, with a glance back at me, disappears behind it.

The curtain is flanked by two men in black. One I recognize as the thug that turned up with Mika. I stride toward them, and one of them puts out a hand to stop me.

"Private guests only."

He's eyeing me like he'd have no problem chucking me out of this place, which wouldn't solve anything for Emily.

I lean in until I'm close to his ear.

"Tell Mika I've come to pay off Krystle's debts."

That'll get his attention.

The man slips behind the curtain, and a few minutes later, he reappears.

"Go through and up the stairs."

Behind the curtain is a line of private booths, some with the curtains drawn and some without. There's the sound of female laughter and the low rumble of male voices.

I can't bear the thought of Emily working in a place like this, and I take the stairs two at a time to get away from it.

Mika's got a glass office on the mezzanine floor that overlooks the club. He beckons me in with a smile that doesn't reach his eyes.

"Ah, Krystle's concerned neighbor. What can I do for you?"

He offers me a seat but I keep standing, eyeing him, sizing him up. Mika's in a tight suit and the same white snakeskin boots he seems to favor. His hands sparkle with more jewelry than a man should wear.

He's got money, and he's got it from the backs of other people.

I pull out an envelope from my pocket and chuck it down on the coffee table. "Krystle's debt."

Mika eyes the envelope hungrily.

"You add the interest?"

"Count it if you like."

He snatches the envelope off the table and flicks through the bills. With some gentle probing, I got out of Emily what she owes.

It seemed like an impossible sum to Emily, especially with the interest accruing weekly.

But I've got money sitting around not doing anything. I live simply; I don't need much. What better way to spend my Army compensation than on the woman I love? Because yeah, as stupid as it sounds, I'm in love with Emily.

Mika smiles, a slow smile like a snake, satisfied the money's all there.

"Congratulations. You just bought yourself a whore."

My fist slams into his face before I know what I'm doing. He stumbles backward, holding his nose, blood spurting all over his white suit.

"What the fuck?"

"No one calls Emily a whore."

The door opens behind me, and I know without looking it's his thugs.

I turn as quickly as my bulky frame will let me, just in time to block a punch. But there's another guy coming at me, and I get a fist to the gut.

Doubled over, I slam my elbow upwards and hear the satisfying sound of cartilage breaking.

"Get the fuck out of my club," Mika screams. And I don't have to be told twice.

I'm practically thrown down the stairs, and I stagger through the corridor, accidentally pulling one of the curtains down.

A woman screams, and suddenly there are people surrounding me as they try to get out of the private booths.

The noise is too loud—the screaming like civilians caught in the crossfire. Suddenly I can't breathe. The noise and pressing bodies are too much. I double over and hold my ears, sucking in long, deep breaths.

One of the thugs shoves me from behind, and that gets me moving. I push through the main curtains and into the bar. Staggering to the doorway, I make it out into the fresh air. My body sucks big breaths into my lungs.

I don't see the punch coming, a parting gift from one of the thugs. It catches me in the nose, and blood spurts out all over my shirt.

"If I see you back here again, you'll get worse than that."

He doesn't need to threaten me. There's no way I'm coming back to this place. Holding my nose, I stagger to my pickup and into the driver's seat.

Then I get the fuck away from there as quickly as I can. All I can think of is getting back to my mountain. Back to Emily.

14
EMILY

The roaring fire and woolen blanket can't stop the cold dread that's set in on my heart. I've been thinking about Mika and his threat, that he'll be back in a week to collect his money. I've seen what he does to people he can't collect from. It was foolish to think I could come out here and he wouldn't find me.

It was foolish to think I could buy enough time to sell the property. I'm going to have to go back to the club and dance.

The thought makes my stomach clench.

I did what I had to do to pay for Dad's medical bills. I thought I could escape the club for good. But I was stupid to think it would be that easy.

"You want another coffee?"

Jenny sets her knitting needles down and runs her hands over her belly. She looks tired, like she's the one who should be resting.

"You don't have to stay, you know. I'll be fine."

Jenny yawns, lifting her arms in a long stretch.

"I gave Sam my word I'd stay 'til he got back." She frowns

and peers at something out the window. "That might be him now."

I follow her gaze to see a pickup truck kicking up a cloud of dust along the road.

My heart leaps in my chest. I didn't realize how happy I'd be to see Sam back.

Jenny picks up her balls of knitting and stuffs them into her bag.

"Thank you for looking out for me," I say.

She smiles warmly.

"Come up and see us sometime."

I feel like I've made a genuine friend today. It makes me sad to think I'll have to leave the mountain just when I'm settling in.

A few minutes later, Sam comes in the door. When I see him, my stomach drops. There's dried blood on his shirt and in his beard.

I leap out of my chair. "What happened?"

Sam holds up his hands. "I'm all right. Looks worse than it is."

"It looks bad," Jenny scolds. "Let me clean you up."

She sets her bag down, and I put my hand on her shoulder.

"You go, Jenny. I'll take care of this."

A look passes between us, like she understands that Sam's my man to look after. Which is weird because he's not really, although I wish he was.

"Call me if you need anything else." Jenny shoulders her bag and gives me a squeeze on the arm and a warm smile before leaving.

She shuts the door behind her, and then it's just me and Sam. I suddenly feel awkward with just the two of us, like I want to hug him and hold him but I don't have that right.

"I'll get some water." I make myself busy to hide the awkwardness.

Sam takes a seat by the fire while I run some warm water. I find a first aid kit under the sink and bring it over to the coffee table beside the couch.

"You want to tell me what happened?"

Crouching next to Sam, I dab a towel into the hot water and wipe at the blood on his face. Sam winces.

"I went to see Mika."

My hand stops halfway back to the bowl.

If he went to see Mika, he knows where Mika is, and he'll have figured out where I used to work. My hand starts shaking, and I dip the towel in the hot water to try to hide the trembling.

"What did you do that for?" My voice comes out as a whisper, and I can't look Sam in the eye. He knows what I am now. A stripper in a seedy club. I'm not the nice girl next door he thought I was.

"I paid off your debt."

The words knock the breath out of me. "You did what?"

I have to hear it again to be sure. No one's ever done anything like that for me before, and I can't comprehend what he's saying.

"I paid your debts. You don't owe that scumbag a thing."

I must be staring at him with my mouth open because Sam chuckles.

"Don't look so shocked. I have money to spare, and I wanted to help."

"Did he do this to you?"

Sam shrugs. "One of his thugs did. I don't think Mika does his own dirty work."

My hand goes to my mouth. I've caused Sam to get beaten up and he's paid off my debt. This man is too kind, too generous.

There must be something else he wants.

My eyes narrow. "Why did you do that?"

Sam shakes his head slowly.

"You don't owe me anything, Emily. I wanted to help and I helped. You're free now to do whatever you want without that scumbag hanging over you."

It takes a moment for the words to truly sink in.

I'm free.

I don't have to dance for money. I don't have to go back to Seattle. I don't have to sell the farm if I don't want to.

The thought sends a tingle down my spine.

What if I could stay here for good, stay here on the mountain with Sam?

He's looking down at me, his beard slick where I've washed off the blood, his lips turned up in a smile. I don't know if I'm stupid because I've already tried to kiss him twice, but hey, third time's the charm.

I sit up on my knees and this time, when I lean in, he meets me halfway.

Sam's kiss is firm and solid, just like him. His hands slide around the back of my neck and wrap in my hair. Sam's hands on me and the press of his lips against mine ignite a fire in me, sending heat through my body. There's a tug deep in my core. A need for him. A sensation I haven't felt before.

Then I remember what I am, a stripper, and how undeserving I am of this man.

I pull away and sit back on my knees. My lips tingle from the kiss, but I can't look at him.

"Hey." Sam tilts my chin up with his hand. "What's the matter?"

He's forcing me to look at him, and his gaze is intense and open. I take a deep breath. I need to confront this head-on.

"Did you find Mika at the club?"

Sam nods slowly. I jerk my head away, unable to look Sam in the eye.

"So, you saw where I worked."

I swallow hard, waiting for his judgment. But Sam doesn't say anything. After a few moments, I steal a glance at him.

Sam's watching me carefully.

"Yeah, I saw what you had to do to look after yourself and your dad."

He looks sad, and I guess that's because he's realizing what I am.

"It was a brave thing to do."

My breath hitches. I search his face, but there's no disgust there. No judgment.

"I hated working there. But the money was good."

God, it sounds bad putting it like that. But there aren't that many options for a girl with no qualifications and big bills to pay.

Sam's hand reaches out and closes over mine.

"You did what you had to do, Emily, but that doesn't define who you are."

His hand is warm as it closes over mine, and I look into his eyes.

There's no judgment. There's no disgust. There's none of the lustful hungriness that I'd see in the men in the club.

What I see in Sam is warmth and understanding and compassion. And in that moment, I think I fall in love.

15
SAM

"Thank you," Emily whispers, and her look is so vulnerable, so broken. I hate the world that has done this to her, that has made a young woman so heartsore.

My hand runs up her arm, and I pull her toward me and up onto the couch.

"You've got nothing to thank me for, honey."

I run my thumb over her cheek, needing to touch her, needing to comfort her. The skin's so soft, so smooth compared to my rough hands.

"Thank you for understanding," she says.

I understand more than she knows. I understand what people do to protect their loved ones. How the person who comes back from war isn't always the same one that left. What families have to go through.

Emily leans against my chest, and we stay like this for a moment. The press of her body against mine is so comforting, reminding me I'm not alone in this world.

After a few moments, Emily's hand slides along my thigh, putting my nerve endings on high alert.

Her hand moves up my thigh, and I suppress a groan as my dick hardens.

"You don't have to do this to thank me."

I place my hand on hers, but she doesn't stop.

"I'm not doing this to thank you. I'm doing this because I want to."

Her hand reaches the top of my jeans and runs over the bulge of my cock, making me rock hard.

Turning to her, she looks up at me, a shy smile on her face. It makes her look even more beautiful.

My mouth closes over hers. She tastes like sweet coffee and citrus and everything good. Our tongues tangle as we explore each other, the sensation sending a buzz through my body.

It's been a long time since I've been with a woman, and never one I cared about the way I do about Emily.

My hands slide around her neck, tangling in her thick hair. I want to feel every part of her, taste all of her.

She moves from her position next to me and climbs onto my lap, one leg on either side, straddling me.

Her hips grind against my bulge, and my dick strains under my pants to get out.

Her hands go to my belt, and with all the restraint I can muster, I put my hands over hers, halting her progress. She looks up at me with a disappointed frown that's fucking adorable. But I need to make sure she's doing this because she wants to, not out of a feeling of obligation.

"Emily, are you sure?"

She nods. "I want this, Sam. I want you. All of you."

The words make me groan with need. I want her more than anything. But not like this.

My hands go to her hips, and I lift her up as I stand up off the couch.

"What are you doing?" she squeals.

"I'm all bloody, sweetheart. I need a shower." Disappointment sweeps over her face. "And you're coming with me."

Hoisting her over my shoulder, I carry her to the bathroom. I set her down gently on the bathmat, her body sliding against mine on the way down.

While we wait for the water to get hot, I undo my buttons and pull my bloodied shirt off. Emily's eyes go wide, and I like the way her gaze roves over my body.

"I've never done this before, Sam." Her voice comes out croaky. She's nervous.

"You never had a shower with anyone?"

She shakes her head slowly and bites her lower lip.

"I've never, you know, done it with anyone."

16
EMILY

Sam stares at me so long I wonder if I've grown two heads. Finally, his mouth twitches into a smile.

"You're a virgin?"

"Yeah." I wince, not sure if it's a good thing. But Sam's smile widens into a mischievous look.

"Oh, honey, you're about to have the best time of your life."

I raise my eyebrows. "If you do say so yourself…"

I don't get to finish my sentence because Sam lifts up my top and slides his hand into my bra. He tugs at my nipples with just the right amount of pressure, making me gasp as a bolt of electricity shoots through my body.

He chuckles at my wide eyes. "Wait 'til I get my tongue on your tits."

His gravelly voice talking dirty like that makes my knees weak. Suddenly I can't wait to get in the shower.

Sam peels his pants off, and I shyly drop my leggings. I've done this at the club a hundred times, but it feels different in front of Sam. It feels more intimate.

I'm glad he didn't question me being a virgin. There were

many times at the club when I could have lost my virginity. Loads of girls did for extra cash.

But I held on to mine. It was the one thing I could hold on to. Stripping was just showing off my body. No one got to penetrate my armor.

Now as I look at Sam's naked body, I lick my lips, thinking about him penetrating me.

His cock sticks out hard and thick, sending both a shock and a bolt of unease through me. "I don't know if you'll fit."

He chuckles, a low sound, close to my ear. "I'll warm you up nice and good."

Sam peels my t-shirt off and unhooks my bra. The cool air hits my nipples and they're instantly hard.

Sam's warm mouth closes over my left nipple, and I gasp at the sensation. Heat zips through my body, accumulating in a single point between my legs.

There's an ache in my pussy that needs release.

"'Sam…" I whisper.

His eyes meet mine, and he seems to know what I need. Without saying a word, he takes my hand and leads me into the shower.

The warm water hits my nipples. A shudder courses through me. The shower doesn't quite fit us both and Sam presses his body against mine. His hard cock pushes against me, and I part my thighs, letting him slide between my legs, his shaft grazing my wet folds.

Sam gets some shower gel on his hands and runs it over my chest, slowly working down to my breasts. A lather builds, making his movements slick as his hands slip and slide all over me.

His mouth meets mine as his hands tug at my nipples, his cock sliding against my pussy lips.

My whole body is on fire and there's a tightness building in my core. My skin prickles as Sam's mouth moves down my throat. The water washes away the soap as his mouth travels over my body. His teeth tug at my nipples, and I gasp at the sensation.

It's almost too much. I feel out of control and needy at the same time. Then he sinks to his knees.

"What are you doing?"

My hands goes to his shoulders and he looks up at me, blinking as water streams over his face.

"Spread your legs."

I don't need to be told twice. Sam takes my knee and places it on one shoulder. I'm wide open. I feel vulnerable, but I trust Sam. A moment later, his mouth closes on my pussy. Heat pulses through me, and I buck my hips.

Sam grabs my ass and pulls my pussy toward him. His tongue slides into me, making me gasp. It's almost too much, this new sensation. But even as I buck my hips away, I know I want more. Sam holds me in place, his tongue relentlessly licking every part of me.

My hard nub is so sensitive that I think I might explode with every stroke of his tongue. My nipples ache and I slide my hands to my breasts, twirling my nipples, tugging on them as Sam licks me.

He glances up, and when he sees me playing with my breasts, his eyes widen and he grunts. His tongue moves faster and now, instead of bucking away, I'm pressing my pussy into his face. Shamelessly rubbing against his face, dragging myself along his rough tongue.

I drop one nipple and grab the back of his head, pulling his face toward me, wanting him to go deeper.

The pressure builds and then it's too much. The ball of energy that's been building under his tongue explodes. Shock waves course through my body. Energy zaps through me from the tiny point in my core all the way to my nipples, my fingertips, my toes. Even the hairs on my head feel energized.

I come apart, shattered by the orgasm that racks through my body. I scream out Sam's name as he keeps his tongue still but pressed against me, the pressure of his tongue becoming the focal point for my orgasm. Everything that I am is squeezed into that one point of pleasure.

I feel alive and free, like there's nothing else in this world at the moment except for the two of us.

Slowly, my body puts itself back together, and I come floating back to Earth. Sam eases the pressure off my clit and sits back on his knees.

His look is hungry, and even though I'm shattered apart, I want more. His hard cock sticks out between his legs, making my pussy throb.

Sam stands up and wipes the water from his eyes. His cock slides into the space between my legs, and I close my thighs around him. His length slips along the folds of my pussy, all juiced up and slick.

He's not even inside me and already I feel the pressure building. The friction of his cock pressing against my clit is working me into a frenzy of need.

I pull at his hair, writhing against him, bucking my hips and grinding into the length of his cock.

Sam's mouth travels down my throat and over my breasts. Teeth graze my nipple, and they're so sensitive that my entire body bucks.

His hand grabs my ass, pulling me against him.

"That's good, honey. You rub yourself on my cock."

I may not have had sex before, but I do know his cock is supposed to be inside me, not rubbing against my outside. But the pleasure I'm experiencing is so overwhelming that I don't care.

"Sam, I think I'm gonna come again."

"Good," he moans. "Come for me, Emily."

And I explode. A shock wave pulses through my body, jolting my bones and shaking my insides.

I didn't think it was possible, but this one is even bigger than the last. I cling to Sam, needing something to center me as I ride the wave of my orgasm.

Sam holds me close until I've stopped shaking. Then he kisses me gently.

"How was that?"

It was good, but I want more. I want so much more. Taking his cock in my palm, I stroke it with a firm hand.

Sam groans, and I feel a deep satisfaction that I can make him do that.

"I want you inside me."

His eyes flick open and they're full of desire. His hungry mouth devours mine, and he brings his hands to my hips.

In one swift movement, he lifts me up onto the shelf of the shower. My thighs fall open, spreading myself for him and inviting him in.

Sam positions his cock at my throbbing entrance. I hold him with both hands, guiding him between my folds.

When I feel his tip inside me, it's like my entire body comes alive. A guttural moan escapes my lips, and it's a sound I don't recognize, like it came from some wild animal.

"You ready, honey?"

"Oh yeah." He thrusts in hard, and there's a shooting pain inside me. My face screws up and Sam stops.

"You okay?"

I nod, trying to breathe. The pain is replaced by a sensation like nothing I've felt before. A fullness, like a piece of the puzzle has been put in place. Like I'm complete.

Sam moves gently, rocking me slowly, until all I feel is pleasure. My hips buck against him and he begins to thrust harder.

He moves slowly at first as he watches my pussy slide up and down the length of his shaft. Then faster. The pressure builds again, and I grab his shoulder, waiting for the wave of pleasure to break.

Just when I think I can't stand it anymore, my orgasm crashes through me. I cry out Sam's name and feel him thicken inside me.

We come together, our worlds exploding around each other. I feel like I've shattered into a million separate pieces, and when we're put back together again, it's as one.

17
SAM

The room is blanketed in a thick smoke. My nostrils crinkle at the smell of burning rubber. Someone's burning a tire somewhere and using the black smoke to hinder our view. The fumes make it almost impossible to breathe.

Machine-gun fire sparks around us, but the smoke warps the sound, making it hard to know which direction it's coming from.

The soldier next to me—a young man, though more of a boy, really—coughs, looking panicked. I signal to move outside. We need to make it to the roof.

He follows me out and we duck down, trying to see past the thick smoke.

There's a ladder on the side of the building, and I grasp a rung, hoisting my body onto it.

There's the sound of rapid fire, and a bullet grazes my helmet, chipping the wall behind me.

"Retreat!" I yell, but the young soldier isn't moving. His body slumps and falls forward.

"No!"

My yell is lost in the smoke.

More soldiers are streaming through the door, trying to get outside.

"It's an ambush!" But my warning is too late.

There's the sound of more gunfire, and I throw my hand over my head, ducking for cover.

A figure comes out of the smoke, and then hands are on me. I swipe at them, beating them off.

"Sam…"

There's a satisfying thump as my arm connects with the enemy.

"Sam…"

The voice is soft, feminine.

"Sam, wake up."

My eyes fly open.

Emily's shaking me awake. My heart's racing, and it takes me a moment to realize where I am.

The dream fades slowly. I'm not in Afghanistan. I'm at home in my cabin with Emily next to me.

"You were having a nightmare."

Emily's face is all concern. She presses a hand to her lip, and her fingers come away with blood on the tips.

"Oh shit." It dawns on me what I've done. "Did I hit you?"

She sits back. "You were thrashing in your sleep."

Ah man, I thrashed around and hit her in the face. After everything she's been through.

"I'm so sorry, Emily."

"It's fine."

She gets up from the bed and pads to the bathroom.

It's not fine. It's far from fine. I've hit her in the face and broken the skin of her lip. How long before I do more damage?

She comes back with a glass of water and holds it out to me. "You want to talk about it?"

She's not mad. She's not even frightened. She's concerned,

and that tugs at my heart. I find I want to open up to Emily. Tell her what I've been through.

"I've not been the same since I got out of the military."

She nods her understanding. It's a scenario she knows too well.

"I have flashbacks, bad dreams, anxiety..."

I run a hand over my eyes. It's hard telling her this, admitting my weaknesses.

"Are you getting any help?" she asks gently.

What can I tell her? Counseling involves going into the city, and I hate going into the city.

"I've got the mountain. I find it calming."

I realize how lame that sounds. How lame I am. I'm a grown man who can't face being around too many people. It's what her dad obviously had. And that caused her enough heartache. She doesn't need that from me.

"You should probably go."

Her brow furrows. "Are you kicking me out in the middle of the night?"

"No. But you deserve someone better than me. You deserve someone whole."

Emily takes my hand in hers and turns it over in her palms.

"We're both broken, Sam." Her hands close around mine. "Maybe together we can make a whole."

Her eyes meet mine, and there's steely determination in her look. She's not scared to be with me. She's not afraid of the challenges we'll face.

There's a stinging sensation behind my eyes and I look away quickly. Goddamn. It's one thing to admit your weaknesses to a woman, it's another to cry in front of her.

Emily climbs into bed next to me and kisses my eyelids and the salty tears threatening there.

"We could both do with a bit of healing, Sam."

I put my arm around her, and some of the heaviness that I

carry around seems to lift. Maybe she's right. Maybe we can heal each other.

"Don't sleep with your watch on, though," she says. "That thing could be lethal."

I glance at the heavy watch on my wrist and am filled with guilt.

"Is this what split your lip?"

"Caught me right here." She taps a spot on her lip, and I kiss it gently.

"I'm so sorry, honey. This thing is staying off."

I take my watch off, and we settle into bed. Emily lies on her side and I press my body against her back. With Emily by my side, I can see a future. It may be challenging, but there is hope.

18

EMILY

*T*he sky is slowly turning light when I slip out of bed, being careful not to wake Sam. I pad to the kitchen and make myself a pot of coffee. As the sun rises over the mountain, I watch the sky change from gray to pink to pale blue.

I passed a restless night thinking about Sam, my dad, and all the other service men and women out there who come back broken.

The light on the mountain changes, and as I watch the trees turn golden, I let out a long sigh. There's something so healing about the mountain, about where we are. If only we could share it with other people.

An idea starts to form in my mind. I sit up straight, thinking of the possibilities.

Searching around Sam's living room, I find some paper and a pen and start making notes.

"You've been busy."

I jump at the sound of Sam's voice. I'm not sure how long

he's been standing there watching me. I've been so engrossed in what I'm doing that I didn't notice him.

"What ya up to?" He indicates the sheets of paper strewn across the coffee table with my scribbled handwriting and crude sketches on them.

"I had an idea." I can't hide the excitement in my voice.

Sam takes a seat next to me and picks up one of the papers. He frowns as he tries to make sense of my drawing.

"It's the old barn." I turn the paper sideways. "I'm trying to figure out how many it could sleep if I converted it into a dormitory."

Sam raises his eyebrows. "What are you planning?"

I bite my bottom lip. Ever since I thought of this idea about an hour ago, I've had a tingle of excitement in the bottom of my spine. But if I say it out loud, it might sound like an utterly ridiculous idea.

"I was thinking about how cool it would be if I could turn my farm into a recovery center for returning veterans."

My pulse is racing as I wait for Sam to speak.

I'm sure he's going to tell me it's a stupid idea. All the way out here in the middle of nowhere? And I've got no experience running a place like that, not to mention the work that's involved in building the damn thing.

He takes a deep breath. I hold mine.

"That's an amazing idea."

The tingle in my spine increases.

"Could it really work?" I ask.

I don't realize I'm nibbling on the end of my pen until a piece of plastic breaks off in my mouth.

Sam looks at my crude drawings and scribbles, really looking at them this time.

"The barn could either be separate living quarters or a few dorms, which would fit more people." I point out two different drawings based on the measurements I've been taking for the real estate agent. "The outbuildings could be counseling rooms. There could be a physiotherapy center with treatment rooms."

Sam's nodding his head. "There're hiking trails around here and good fishing spots."

He's as excited about this as I am.

"You could have cooking classes," he adds.

I furrow my brow. "Why cooking classes?"

"Because for some men, the Army is all they've known. They've never had to do things for themselves, like cook. Not having those basic life skills can really hinder the transition to civilian life, especially if you're dealing with PTSD on top of that."

He scribbles a few things down on a piece of paper. I'm thrilled that he's as excited about this as I am, that it's not just a stupid idea.

Then a thought occurs to me.

"I don't know how I'd fund it all. It'll cost a fortune to convert the old farm into the kind of facility we need."

Sam sits back on the couch. "Leave that bit to me."

"What do you mean?"

"I've got some money I can put toward this."

I start to protest, and he holds his hand up. "There're also grants we can get. A lot of people would be willing to donate. We can get loans to finance the development and donations to keep it running."

"Do you really think it will work?"

Sam shrugs. "I dunno, but it's a brilliant idea. You want to give it a go?"

His eyes shine with excitement. And I think if I could help even just one person like Sam, then it will be worthwhile.

"Yeah. I do."

Sam grins at me. "Then let's do it."

EPILOGUE

EMILY

Five years later…

The deep, rumbly tones of my husband's singing reach me through the bedroom door.

"Dadda."

Twilla wriggles her small body around and sits up in the bed. One small foot kicks out, and I cover my belly protectively. The baby kicks as it feels my touch, pressing itself against my hand.

"Dadda sing."

Twilla giggles and climbs over my face to get out of the bed, putting an end to any last hope I had of getting more sleep.

She climbs carefully off the bed, backward and feet first, just as Sam comes out of the ensuite bathroom.

"Hey, little one."

Sam scoops her into his arms, and she giggles as he throws her into the air.

"It's a bit early, isn't it?" I say.

The baby has been moving inside me all night, and at some

point, Twilla joined us in the bed. Between her and the baby, I haven't had the best sleep.

Sam comes around to the side of the bed and kisses my forehead.

"We've got new arrivals coming this morning," he says.

The rest and rehabilitation center opened three years ago, and to say it's given my husband a new lease on life is an understatement.

Sam runs the place with pride and compassion, getting to know every single man and woman who passes through.

Today his beard is freshly clipped, his outfit freshly pressed. I watch with pride as my husband dresses.

He usually does the meet-and-greet. As an ex-serviceman, Sam's the frontman of the center. I stay behind the scenes and look after the general management of the place.

I slide my feet over the edge of the bed and, with a hand on my round belly, slowly get up. I'm due in a few weeks' time, and getting around is beginning to feel awkward.

Sam throws Twilla on the bed and she opens her little arms. "Again, again."

I leave them giggling together as I make my way to the kitchen. The sky is just starting to turn pink, and I pause to watch the sunrise.

Sam comes up behind me and slides a hand around my waist. I lean against him as he kisses my neck.

Together we watch the sun creep up the valley, casting everything in a golden light.

It's a healing light. I've seen firsthand the healing power of the mountain. But I know it's not just the mountain. It's the people who work with us and help those who are broken mend their bodies, minds, and hearts.

When I came to Maple Mountain, I was broken too. My years with Sam have been the happiest of my life. It hasn't always been easy, but we healed each other. And together we are whole.

MOUNTAIN MAN'S OBSESSION

His one obsession is her...

From the moment Colette sweeps into my bar, I can't stop watching her. Even when she doesn't know I'm looking. *Especially* then.
My cameras record her every smile, every frown, every moment. I study her until I know my girl inside out, my obsession growing, overwhelming me, demanding I act.

She'll never find out my secret, will she?

Mountain Man's Obsession features an OTT obsessed mountain man and the curvy innocent woman he claims as his own. It's high heat, oh so sweet, and always with a happily ever after.

Check it out here:
mybook.to/MMObsession

BOOKS BY SADIE KING

Series set on the Sunset Coast
Underground Crows MC
Sunset Security
Men of the Sea
The Thief's Lover

Series set in Maple Springs
Men of Maple Mountain
All the Single Dads
Candy's Café
Small Town Sisters

Series set in Kings County
Kings of Fire
King's Cops

For more of Sadie King's books check out her website
www.authorsadieking.com

GET YOUR FREE BOOK

Sign up to the Sadie King mailing list for a FREE book!

You'll be the first to hear about exclusive offers, bonus content and all the news from Sadie King.

To claim your free book visit:
www.authorsadieking.com/free

Follow Sadie King on BookBub to get an alert whenever she has a new release, preorder, or discount!

bookbub.com/authors/sadie-king

Printed in Great Britain
by Amazon